Mr. Panda's Painting

written and illustrated by
Anne Rockwell

Macmillan Publishing Company   New York

Maxwell Macmillan Canada   Toronto

Maxwell Macmillan International   New York   Oxford   Singapore   Sydney

For Nicholas, Julianna, and Nigel

Macmillan Publishing Company, 866 Third Avenue, New York, NY 10022.
Maxwell Macmillan Canada, Inc., 1200 Eglinton Avenue East, Suite 200,
Don Mills, Ontario M3C 3N1.
First edition
Printed in the United States of America
10 9 8 7 6 5 4 3 2 1
The text of this book is set in 24 pt. Barcelona Book.
The illustrations are rendered in silk screen on canvas with acrylics.

Library of Congress Cataloging-in-Publication Data
Rockwell, Anne F.
   Mr. Panda's painting / written and illustrated by Anne Rockwell. — 1st ed.
      p.   cm.
   Summary: Mr. Panda, an artist, buys tubes of paint in every color and then
goes home and paints a picture with them.
   ISBN 0-02-777451-1
   [1. Color—Fiction.   2. Artists—Fiction.   3. Pandas—Fiction.]
I. Title.   II. Title: Mister Panda's painting.
PZ7.R5943Mr   1993   [E]—dc20   92-9220

3/17/94

Mr. Panda was an artist
who painted pictures all day long.
But one day he used up all his paint,

so he had to buy some more.

He bought a tube of red paint and a tube of blue.
Then he bought a tube of yellow paint
and a tube of orange.
Soon he saw his favorite shade of green

and he bought that, too.
Then Mr. Panda remembered
that he liked purple, as well.
So he bought a tube of purple paint.

As Mr. Panda walked down the street
carrying his new tubes of paint
he saw something very beautiful.
It was red,
just like the tube of red paint
in his shopping bag.

Then Mr. Panda saw something as blue
as the new tube of blue paint
in his shopping bag.

But no sooner had Mr. Panda seen
such beautiful red and blue things
than he saw something as yellow
as the tube of yellow paint
in his shopping bag.
He thought the yellow daffodils
were so beautiful he bought a bouquet.

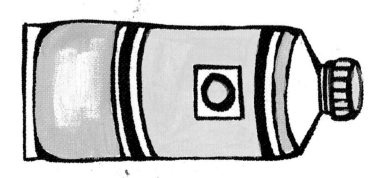

Mr. Panda continued on his way,
thinking what a lot
of bright and beautiful things
there were in the world.
He was thinking about the painting
he could make
with all his new tubes of paint.

When Mr. Panda crossed the street
he saw some things that were orange.
They were as orange
as the big, fat tube of orange paint
that was in his shopping bag.
"I like orange!" Mr. Panda said.

Soon Mr. Panda saw many other things
that were red, blue, yellow, and orange.

He couldn't decide which color he loved most.
They were all so bright and beautiful.

Mr. Panda turned the corner and came
to a street all lined with trees.
The trees were covered with leaves of green.
It was so cool under those leaves of green
that Mr. Panda decided green was surely
the most beautiful color of all.

The trees all covered with
leaves of green were so beautiful
Mr. Panda decided to paint
a picture of them
as soon as he got home.
Suddenly it began to rain.

Mr. Panda did not
want to get wet.
He did not want his
new tubes of paint
to get wet.
So he began
to run.

The rain came down harder.

"Mr. Panda! Mr. Panda!" someone called.

It was his neighbor.

"Come share my umbrella with me," she said.

"Then you won't get all wet."

"What a nice color purple is," said Mr. Panda
as he ran under her beautiful purple umbrella.

"And I almost forgot to buy some!"

When Mr. Panda got home he put
the yellow daffodils in a blue pitcher
and stood them on the old green table.
A red apple and a juicy orange
were on the table, too.
"But something is missing," said Mr. Panda.
He went over to his comfortable armchair
so he could sit down to look and think.

A book was lying in the armchair.
It was purple.
"That is exactly what I need!"
said Mr. Panda.
"I need some purple in my painting."
So he put the purple book
on the old green table.
Then he put the red apple on the purple book.

Everything looked just perfect to him.
Mr. Panda put the new tubes of paint
on the taboret next to his easel.
He put on his blue smock.

He squeezed some green paint onto his palette.
Then Mr. Panda picked up his brush

and
made
his
painting.